HORRISGROWSDOWN

By
Shari Becker

Illustrated by
Valeria Petrone

G. P. PUTNAM'S SONS

For Pat, who believed in me and my voice
–S. B.

To Umberto for inspiration and fun
–V. P.

G. P. PUTNAM'S SONS
A division of Penguin Young Readers Group.
Published by The Penguin Group.
Penguin Group (USA) Inc., 375 Hudson Street, New York, NY 10014, U.S.A.
Penguin Group (Canada), 90 Eglinton Avenue East, Suite 700, Toronto, Ontario,
Canada M4P 2Y3 (a division of Pearson Penguin Canada Inc.).
Penguin Books Ltd, 80 Strand, London WC2R 0RL, England.
Penguin Ireland, 25 St. Stephen's Green, Dublin 2, Ireland (a division of Penguin Books Ltd.).
Penguin Group (Australia), 250 Camberwell Road, Camberwell, Victoria 3124, Australia
(a division of Pearson Australia Group Pty Ltd).
Penguin Books India Pvt Ltd, 11 Community Centre, Panchsheel Park, New Delhi - 110 017, India.
Penguin Group (NZ), Cnr Airborne and Rosedale Roads, Albany, Auckland 1310, New Zealand
(a division of Pearson New Zealand Ltd).
Penguin Books (South Africa) (Pty) Ltd, 24 Sturdee Avenue, Rosebank, Johannesburg 2196, South Africa.
Penguin Books Ltd, Registered Offices: 80 Strand, London WC2R 0RL, England.

Text copyright © 2007 by Shari Becker. Illustrations copyright © 2007 by Valeria Petrone.
All rights reserved. This book, or parts thereof, may not be reproduced in any form without permission
in writing from the publisher, G. P. Putnam's Sons, a division of Penguin Young Readers Group,
345 Hudson Street, New York, NY 10014. G. P. Putnam's Sons, Reg. U.S. Pat. & Tm. Off.
The scanning, uploading and distribution of this book via the Internet or via any other means
without the permission of the publisher is illegal and punishable by law. Please purchase only authorized
electronic editions, and do not participate in or encourage electronic piracy of copyrighted materials.
Your support of the author's rights is appreciated. The publisher does not have any control over and
does not assume any responsibility for author or third-party websites or their content.

Published simultaneously in Canada. Manufactured in China by South China Printing Co. Ltd.
Design by Gina DiMassi. Text set in Berliner Grotesk Medium. The illustrations were digitally rendered.
Library of Congress Cataloging-in-Publication Data
Becker, Shari. Horris grows down / by Shari Becker ; illustrated by Valeria Petrone.
p.   cm.   Summary: Not knowing what else to do with their enormous son, four-year-old Horris,
his parents find him a job in a box factory, where he works hard and tries his best but still does not fit in.
[1. Child labor–Fiction. 2. Parent and child–Fiction. 3. Giants–Fiction.] I. Petrone, Valeria, ill. II. Title.
PZ7.B381715Hor 2007 [E]–dc22   2006009155   ISBN 978-0-399-24358-5
1 3 5 7 9 10 8 6 4 2
First Impression

Horris Zeldnik was born big.
The doctors said they'd never seen a baby that large.

Horris was so big that his mother had
to stand on her tiptoes to rock his cradle
and she had to climb on eleven books
just to kiss him good night.

"Horris is so big!" said his father.
"But we must try to treat him like a regular baby."
His mother agreed.
So they got him a stroller and took him out.
But Horris's mother had to push the back wheels
and his father pulled the front.

Horris drank six cartons of milk at each meal, and he had to use a hairbrush to clean his teeth.

And when Horris played
hide-and-seek,
it wasn't very hard to find him.

When Horris was four, he was so big that
his parents didn't know what to do.
"We've tried to treat him like a regular child,"
said his mother. "But he's just too big."

"He is a big guy," agreed his father.
"Maybe he should just get a job."
His mother thought it was a splendid idea.

And so four-year-old Horris put on a bow tie,
packed his red backpack, climbed on his tricycle
and set out in search of a job.

He found the perfect position at
Bernard Backelbass's Box Factory.
"What are your qualifications?"
Backelbass asked in the interview.

"I'm very good at sizes," said Horris.
"I know small, medium and large."
"Perfect," said Backelbass.
"I need someone with just your skills!"

Horris was hired as a box sorter, and he did his job well. Every morning at 7:30, he put on his bow tie, packed his backpack, climbed on his tricycle, rode to work and signed in. Every day he sorted boxes into small, medium and large.

Sometimes he sorted by color, too:
yellow, brown and white.

On very special days,
Backelbass even let Horris
stomp on broken boxes.
He liked that best of all.
Every evening at 5:00,
Horris signed out,
put on his backpack,
climbed on his tricycle and
rode home. His parents
were very pleased.
And so was Horris.

Horris liked the factory. He even made some friends.
But when his coworkers invited him out to
a steakhouse for lunch, he could not go.
"I'm not allowed to use sharp knives," said Horris.
Besides, his mother had already made him ten jelly sandwiches.

They invited him to a party, and he could not go.
"I have to be in bed by seven," he said.
He tried to join his coworkers for a coffee break,
but the coffee tasted awful!

Then one day Backelbass asked Horris to fill in for a missing box counter. Horris could only count to ten and there were many more boxes than that. He kept getting mixed up.

Backelbass was not happy.
"Go home and don't come back until you
can count to 100!" he said.
Horris left with his head hung low.

He had ridden only a few blocks when suddenly—
THWOMP!
An orange rubber ball hit Horris in the head.

"Oops," said a little voice. Horris looked down
and saw a boy standing next to him.
"My ball hit you on the head," he said. "Sorry."
Horris handed the ball back to the boy and
watched him walk away toward the sound of laughter.

Horris decided to follow the boy.
Just around the corner,
children were gathered in a field
next to a big yellow brick building.
Horris watched the boy
throw the ball to a little girl.

"What do you do here?"
he asked the boy.
"We're playing,"
replied the boy.
"Are you well paid?"
Horris asked.
"Huh?" said the boy.

"What are your hours like?" Horris asked the girl.
"What are you talking about?" she asked.
"You're lucky you don't have to wear a bow tie,"
he said to the girl. She shook her head.

"Come play," said the boy.
And he did.

Just as Horris began to feel his tummy rumble, the little girl stood up. "It's snacktime," she said. "I have to go."

"Snacktime?" said Horris. That sounded good.

Horris went home. His mother was surprised to see him in the middle of the day. She was worried he might be sick, but Horris shook his head no. "Mr. Backelbass says I can't count high enough," he said. "Can I have some cookies? It's snacktime."

"I think you're a splendid counter,"
said his mother, and she told him he could eat
as many cookies as he could count.
Horris ate his ten cookies while his mother called
his father and asked him to come home.

"Now, son," said his father.
"Don't feel bad. There are more
box-sorting jobs out there."
Horris just shrugged.
"I don't want to go back to boxes,"
he said. "I found a new job.
Come on, I'll show you!"

Horris took his parents to the playground.
"The pay is nothing," he told them.
"But the hours are great! And you can
have snacks whenever you want!"

"It sounds wonderful," said his mother,
and she kissed him on the head.
"You're perfectly qualified for that position—
and I bet school would be a great fit, too."
"School?" said Horris. "Yes, school.
Maybe they could even teach me to count to 100."